Connolly Rising (Part1)
by Paul Larkin

For Fiona, X.

"May the whores of the empire lie awake in their beds
And sweat as they count out the sins on their heads"

Shane MacGowan, *Streets of Sorrow / Birmingham Six*

'Whores of the Empire'

"Hold on, let me get comfy"

The living room was immaculate, the couch in the same place it had been since the day it was delivered. The television set was dust free as always whilst the coffee table had the white, frilly cotton tablecloth on it that had been bought from John Lewis in St James Centre and the four coasters with The Queen on, each placed at each corner of the table.

The plastic mat, reserved only for special occasions, had been placed in front of the fireplace which was cold on account of it being late and them not being long in from the club. They always went to the club on Hogmanay. It was a good night, everyone was there and the band, *Boyne Again* from Broxburn, had belted out all the classics. Alexander Charles and Victoria Elizabeth McMillan, now back at their cold home, had particularly enjoyed dancing to "*Could you go a*

Chicken supper Bobby Sands" Almost nine years had passed since the IRA hunger striker had died but the hate for him, in that club, remained as strong as ever.

"Right, that feels better"

Sandy C. was comfortable, so Vicky started stripping off as a matter of procedure. They knew the routine as well as the bible. They had been married 29 years, both 20 when they took their vows and had been indulging in this practice for the last 10 years. Everything was by the book in the McMillan household, the bible above all, but the book this procedure came from wasn't the bible. Mid-life crisis they had put it down to. Sandy C. had gone to a big Masonic convention in Rotterdam and, on his arrival in his hotel room on Zuidenwijdsestraat, he began putting his clothes in the wardrobe, mainly a suit and the full masonic regalia of ties, apron badges, medals and cufflinks. It was opening the top drawer of the two-drawer bedside cabinet that he stumbled upon a magazine. Studying it closer, he saw the name was *Gouden Douches Maandelijks* a name that meant nothing to him. Upon closer inspection, Sandy C. saw things he had never seen before.

"Crouch a bit further, I want to see your arsehole as well, hen"

Vicky grimaced a little. At 49, her knees had seen better days, particularly when she had spent a lot of time crouched over her husband's face. It had all started when Sandy C. had come back from that convention in the Netherlands just before Christmas, 1979. Margaret Thatcher had taken power in Great Britain the previous May and not long after, Sandy C. had announced he would be part of a delegation from Edinburgh (Leith Walk to be precise) to go to Rotterdam just before Christmas to be part of a convention of worldwide masons. She was sworn to secrecy of course and, unlike most wives, had no concerns about Sandy C. making it a jolly. He wasn't like that. Well, at least until he came back and showed her the magazine. The result being that every Friday night and special occasions like Hogmanay and Christmas night, they indulged themselves in this ritual. Even though it was Hogmanay, they'd slipped out of the club before the bells on the pretence that Brothers round the world would be phoned and wished "Happy New Year" but in reality, the early taxi back to EH15 (Joppa) was for an ulterior motive.

"Grab it now"

Being a Mason and an Orangeman, Sandy C. was no stranger to rituals. In becoming a Mason in Edinburgh, he rode on a Goat. That means he got on one and it walked him round Masonic hall in George Street, Edinburgh, a place that he rarely frequented unless it was for meetings, he much preferred the cosier and friendlier atmosphere of the

Edinburgh Masonic Club in Shrub Lane. He and Vicky attended the club every Friday night without fail and on special occasions like the Hogmanay do they had just attended. They had implemented this ritual to their club night, indulging themselves, really, for Sandy C. He had been stressed through various issues related to Ireland within the Orange Order and the huge support the Republican Movement had gained through the actions of the very people that Sandy C. and friends had been mocking hours earlier in the club.

"Keep a strong hold of it, Vicky, darling"

Even so, Sandy C. was incredibly young to be suffering from erectile dysfunction. Vicky had tried all sorts to get *Wee Sandy* up and pumping again but to little avail. She had dressed up. Nurses, Naughty School Girls and even once as a Nun (Sandy C. felt even more humiliated by that one, his mind couldn't get off the fact that even the Catholic Church were laughing at him. There was humiliation that got him off and then there was that type of humiliation) Then she tried to talk dirty to him. Lying in bed, she would gently caress his flaccid member and remind him of all the times he had sexually satisfied her. This just made Sandy C. feel worse, like a footballer who came on as a sub in the last 10 minutes to save the game, jinking past defenders before smashing it into the top corner and now he could be barely get up off the bench.

"Put the big finger up, now"

Vicky could relate. Her legs felt like an early retired footballer's. Despite the honing of her routine, it didn't get any easier. She had to take up a precise position or the ritual simply wouldn't work. The saving grace for her was it only lasted two-three minutes, sometimes five if Sandy C. had a good drink in him. Their dog, a black poodle called *Stone*, was young but old enough to ensconce himself in his basket. Sandy C. was a *McEwan's Export* man (Helped that King Billy was on all the cans and advertising) but sometimes he had a flurry of whiskeys before they got a taxi home (There were always 5 or 6 Brothers waiting outside the club ready to ferry the high heid yins home) and he would take longer to climax. He had to be focused though, he was stressed about a few things recently.

"Ok darling, go"

Vicky assumed her position, her left hand was wrapped round Sandy C's soft cock, the middle finger of her right hand was placed up Sandy C's rectum and her flaps opened to allow a deluge of pish to explode on Sandy C's staunch physiognomy. As the urine touched skin, she felt Sandy get harder in her hand and she started pulling his foreskin back and forward, so it got its full erect five inches. Her finger was fully inserted in Sandy C's anus and she was chugging at that hard helmet whilst she had the chance. Sandy C. needed her to have a grip like Geoff Capes to keep in the moment and Vicky rarely let him down as much as *Wee Sandy* had. The stench of pish rarely troubled either of them. Like assistants in a care home, they got used it. This was a good night for Vicky, she felt Sandy C's semen dribble over her hand in less than three minutes giving her the opportunity to get up and get cleaned up.

"Thank you, Victoria"

They cleaned up, Vicky got the products from under the sink in the kitchen and came back in to give the mat a good scrub. Sandy C. went through to the bathroom and turned the shower on. He had not long had it installed by Davie Ferguson who did it for twenty quid and a pint at the club and it saved so much time on these occasions. He felt the water on his face and the gratification wash all over him again. He had to get to bed and get a good night's sleep though, there was football tomorrow. Against the auld enemy.

'Beware of the risen people'

The Tango was bouncing. Revellers were outside too but in the cold. The regulars were being taken care of in the pub, each given a ticket that allowed them to get past the three bouncers on the door (all wearing black bomber jackets, black trousers and black shoes-Unbeknown the public, two had a cosh on them and one had a knuckleduster) and keep the pub at an enjoyable limit. Outside was bedlam. For years now, people headed for The Tron so they could be an Olympian standard of cold as they celebrated a new year coming in. This seemed like lunacy to John Patrick Quinlivan. At just 20, he was already a well kent face in Edinburgh on account of his political activities and beliefs that were anathema to a lot of the population of Edinburgh never mind the rest of Scotland. Closer inspection though revealed that they were worth exploring. Underneath John, and the pub for that matter, there was a long since forgotten plaque that bore witness to the achievements of a man born just down the road. Long forgotten to some but not all. John Quinlivan had sought to change that. In 1986, in the Craigmillar district of Edinburgh, John had organised a march to commemorate the life and work of the man on the small plaque in the Cowgate, James Connolly.

Connolly had been born and bred in Edinburgh but, other than the plaque underneath a bridge in the city's "Little Ireland" there had been very little recognition of the man from Edinburgh City Council or any of its representatives. It's fair to say that their policy towards Connolly was at best ignorance and at worst, embarrassment. There had been various people and the odd, small, campaign who tried to alert the populous to Connolly's achievements, but the minute most heard "Dublin 1916" doors were slammed shut and minds were closed with the same vigour. Then in early 1986, a plan was hatched by a few like-minded folk, and an organisation was formed in Connolly's name. The short-term-plan was to march on the streets of Edinburgh. The long-term plan was to enshrine the name of Connolly into Edinburgh's psyche.

The march took place with around 50 marchers and 200 protestors. It was deemed a success by John in the *Edinburgh Evening News* and this was borne out by the fact that in the subsequent years, despite huge opposition, the march moved to the Grassmarket area of Edinburgh and started to really grow in numbers. The years of 1987, 1988 and 1989 would see protest from Loyalists and right-wing factions but ultimately a growing awareness of Connolly and his work, as well as the political situation in Ireland. Many people made that possible but no one more than John Patrick Quinlivan.

Right now, though, another pint was on John's mind.

"Gimme eh, three lager, a bottle of becks and a pint of heavy please"

John was at the bar of *The Tango*. He drank between here and the boozer a couple of doors down, *Frasier's*, but that had shut at 10pm tonight on account of the landlord and landlady's love of a scoop too. They had long since made their money. He was with his crew of usual suspects from the schemes of Gilmerton, Muirhouse, Niddry and various parts of Leith. He himself was from Gilmerton but was currently residing in Royston Mains Green after his mother and father had split up. His mother had moved outside the city and his father has bought a place in the south side of Edinburgh city centre, which left John with a choice. He chose the council and they had allocated him in a house in an area that he wasn't overly familiar with but had enough comrades in close proximity to feel secure enough.

And that was absolutely crucial.

Since becoming the public face of the campaign to engage people with James Connolly, he had been met with torrents of hatred. There were various loyalist magazines, notably *Red Hand Commando*, that took pleasure in printing his address in its issues. His photograph had appeared in various Orange halls and questions had been asked about "What should we do about this scum?"
There had also been a UVF commander who had been spotted in Edinburgh, a mile or so from John's flat, in a purely coincidental moment by a comrade of John's. The comrade immediately ran to the first phone box he knew and telephoned first John, then his ex-partner, to warn of the presence of one Hillary Rock, a UVF Commander and member of the Progressive Unionist Party. This made John and his group cautious and vigilant but steadfast in their goals of promoting Connolly and uniting Ireland.

Right now, though, drink was on their mind.

The bells went and the usual embraces were made among everyone in the bar. Looks would go around the bar also. For potential enemies sure, but also for friendly female faces. These guys were dedicated political activists, but they were also young men making their way in the world and looking for new discoveries every day.

John caught the eye of a dirty blonde in the bar. Looks were exchanged in that nonchalant but studious way that people show interest but not too much in case they get a knock back. The girl started to move through the bar as if she was being pulled by a tug of war team on Valium. John took a long swig of his lager as he kept one eye on her. He watched as she jinked her way through faster now, like John Collins at Easter Road last week against The Huns, and he knew she was going to speak to him- "Is the toilet this way?" The bathroom was behind John and he nodded back and to his right whilst keeping his eyes locked firmly on hers. This wasn't arrogance, he had already calculated that he would get the unnecessary attention of his company the second he started speaking to her. The look was there though. She brushed past John and went to powder her nose. John watched her walk up the three stairs and knew she was smiling.

"You gawn tae Tynecastle the morn?"

John's moment was interrupted by Seany's question.

"Eh, aye, I got a ticket yesterday, they had 200 left in the Hibs shop on Easter Road. I wisane gonnae go, but I was in Sally's hoose and heard it on *Radio Forth* so I bolted doon and got one"

The traditional Hearts versus Hibs fixture on New Year's Day was being played at Tynecastle this year.

The other traditional fixture, Rangers versus Celtic, was being played at Celtic Park the day after.

Seany Beef was John's right hand man. He had been by his side from the formation of the Connolly organisation. Before that even.

"I'm gawn tae Parkheid on the Leith bus on Tuesday" Seany volunteered.

John's mind was elsewhere though. The dirty blonde was close to being within sniffing range and her perfume was getting closer. As she got parallel with John, another look was exchanged.

John turned to his crew.

"Right boys, big game the morn and I need a kebab, I'll be in touch about the next meeting by the weekend"

With that, John made his move.

'Whores of the Empire'

It was a new year but something of the same old story. The weather was that typical Scottish freezing, windy, raining and dull all in one sitting. The game kicked off at 3pm but already there was a need to have the floodlights on. The night was already creeping in, yet it didn't bother the 25,000 plus in the ground. Far from it. Indeed, a substantial number of the ground was still inebriated from the festivities of the night before. Quite a few hadn't even gone to bed and were now screaming obscenities at no one in particular. There was even the odd fan sat down on the terrace, asleep.

None of these applied to Sandy C. McMillan.

He shuffled along the centre stand, minding his P's and Q's, until he was sat in his seat. Somewhere he had occupied for roughly 10 years since Brother Mercer had bought the club. There was no need for the purchase of a season ticket. All Sandy C. had to do was say his name at the front door. Occasionally, a new press guy would witness this and wonder who Sandy C. was but most of the old guard were brothers and knew the protocols. He would have a pint and a half in the boardroom as was his wont, with handshakes even more to the fore given the date. He would admire Wallace working the room, always making connections and always an air of authority. Wallace's kids, Ian and Helen, were there and Helen had always caught his eye with that chest of hers. For a few seconds, Sandy C. imagined her crouching over him…

The bell went, signalling it was time to go to your seat (A Wallace introduction aimed at the theatre crowd) and this was why Sandy now found himself excusing himself past people he knew and didn't know. Sandy C. was a big noise in Edinburgh circles and people like Wallace Mercer needed him. Mercer may have been a self-made man in the eyes of the public, but the reality was, being a member of the Freemasons had helped him massively. His public utterances reeked of bluster and hubris, but he needed people like Sandy C. to progress. Hearts were in dire financial straits when Wallace Mercer bought the club, so Sandy C. went to work. The cost of Hearts refuse collection was on the high side so Sandy C. put a red pen through that and got three fellow Jambos, and brothers, to collect Hearts rubbish at the end of a shift in exchange for three tickets for a home game. Cost of getting into a home game then was £1. The rubbish bill was £950 a year so Sandy C. did the math. Then there was the catering. Hearts had paid a firm, *Groathill Home Bakery*, to supply food for the boardroom, players and pie stands. However, Sandy C. knew a man. John Martin was a legend in the Pilton area of Edinburgh. He had revolutionised the food delivery business in the 1970's in North Edinburgh when he realised there wasn't a shop open before 12.30pm in the area on a Sunday and no one had the foresight, or will for that matter, to get their rolls on the day before. John (*China* to his friends on account of his resemblance to someone from there) knew a supplier and had the bright idea of getting rolls, and Sunday papers, to take to the masses on a Sunday morning so the populous could continue nursing their hangovers.

It was a huge success.

This was despite John's mode of delivery being on foot with the goods in an old pram that had been for his son, also John, when he was young, but the system worked fine. His marketing and advertising ploy were way ahead of the likes of *Saatchi and Saatchi* who spent hundreds of thousands of pounds on campaigns and Oxbridge-educated people to come up with marketable slogans. China simply took to the streets, with his pram full of rolls and papers and shouted

"ROLLLLLS ROLLLLLLSSSSS N PAAAAAPPPERRRSSSS"

The Pram in front was very much China's.

Sandy C. had given Brother Martin a phone call and, before long, China was supplying Hearts with their rolls, pies, sausage rolls and even *Oxo* cubes that were way cheaper than the standard *Bovril* all clubs sold. In one handshake, China had saved the club £30,000 a year. For this, he was given an unannounced lifetime Presidency of the club, with a letter from Brother Mercer himself, ensuring he would never have to pay for entry into a Hearts match as long as he owned the club. The only stipulation Brother Mercer had made was that, like the Brotherhood, it would remain a secret.

The game began at the usual frenetic pace, with John Collins, carrying on from his good performance in the previous game against Rangers at Easter Road, going close with a chance that Hearts goalkeeper, Henry Smith, did well to save.

The game was petering out towards half time when Neil Cooper inexplicably brought down Wayne Foster in the Gorgie Road end box. Referee Alastair Huett pointed to the spot immediately with Hearts fans gleefully accepting the gift like someone accepting another nip at new year. Sandy C. was up out his seat, everyone staring at each other and commenting on the stupidity of Cooper.

"Foster was going nowhere there!"

"That's a stonewaller!"

"Robbo will bury this!"

John Robertson, the hammer of Hibs, duly stepped up and sent Hibs goalie

Goram, who couldn't save any points today, the wrong way to put Hearts one up, and keep Hibs lowly.

Sandy C. felt triumphant. This was the sort of game which could have gone either way, but Hearts now had a strong grip on. The half time whistle was blown and the great and good of Hearts all started to shuffle back to the hospitality the boardroom offered. The columnist and broadcaster, Gerry McNee, had started poking fun at the people who occupied the hospitality area of Ibrox, calling them *Fat Cats* but Sandy never saw himself like that. Yes, he had great connections through the lodges, both Masonic and Orange, but he saw those as rewards for being a loyal and diligent member of both organisations. Through years of service, he had ended up as the public face of the Orange Order in the Lothians. From around 1970 to the present, any time the press needed a sound bite or some information from an Orange perspective, they phoned Sandy

C. He was comfortable with this position for many years as it went completely unchallenged for a good 15 years.

After swallowing two nips in the boardroom, Sandy returned to his seat just as the Hibs team emerged from the tunnel. Looking down on them, Sandy C's eyes went left to the Gorgie Road end of the ground, a sea of green and white greeting the Hibs team that was heading towards the school end of the ground and Sandy C. had nothing but contempt for the 9000 or so Hibs fans who had come to support their team at Tynecastle. Surveying all the clapping hands and green and white scarves held up in the air, with a quite a lot singing with gusto the anthem *You'll Never Walk Alone* and a few others trying to get the words out whilst having a discreet pish on the terracing, due to the woefully inadequate location of the toilets, Sandy focused on a young boy, 15 maybe 16 and saw him giving the now the emerging from the tunnel Hearts team the traditional "Fuck You" sign with his left hand slapping the middle of his right arm and his right fist, clenched, going up and down.

Sandy focused on the boy, his thoughts almost meditating through his head as everything else cleared their way away from his mind to focus right to the front of his mind and the one word thought that came to the forefront.

"Scum"

'Beware of the risen people'

John was near the bend of the Tynecastle terracing at the Gorgie Road end. He was with a fair squad that stretched all the way to divide between the Hibs support and Hearts support. The squad he was with could politely be described as moody or shady but to others it was fearsome. It would be fair to say that these people, under this guise, had terrorised football grounds and surrounding areas for six years now. They had a well-known name, that, no matter what bravado others portrayed, struck fear into anyone who had a fist in football fighting. Within that though, there was a small, elite group, no more than 20, that formed the core. They were the organisers, the hardest, the generals. John was on the cusp of this group, well respected but ultimately hampered by his political activism not allowing him to attend every game plus meetings of his own to organise for the Connolly boys. However, he had a very good friend that was within this group, known as *The Family*, who had a name that struck the kind of fear that belied his years. Not yet 20, he had forged a reputation in Edinburgh on the canvas and on the streets. (Mind you, it was his opponents who knew the canvas a lot better than him, he had been boxing since he was 13 and had already amassed 200 fights, only losing three on points and never once being knocked down)

When John Robertson ran through early in the second half and swept the ball past Andy Goram to put Hearts 2-0 up, Luke Doyle glanced at John as if to say "They will pay for this" but never said a word. As cavorting Jambos screamed obscenities at *The Family* from the safety of two fences and a tunnel divide, the boys in turn simply smiled and waved back but inside they were burning.

The game petered out as the rain came teeming in. Loads of Hibbys had seen enough and weren't prepared to get soaked as well. *The Family* had also made their move but for different reasons. They fell into rank like well-trained soldiers and were noticeable among the many green and white scarves that were now being used by other fans as protection from the rain.

Just as they got outside of the stadium, next to the church, the final whistle was blown, and a huge cheer was heard from the Hearts areas of the ground. There were around 40 of the top boys now melting into the Hibs support as they turned left on Gorgie Road towards the city centre. They were clad in the best designer gear around, *Stone Island, POP 84* and *Adidas Trimm Trab* were in abundance. The police were trying to keep them separated from the jubilant Jambos who were now emerging from McLeod Street, a few hundred yards up the road. As the Hearts support noticed their grieving rivals, they gloated, they jeered, they laughed. Within that Hearts mob were a few boys, ones that fancied themselves. As the Hibs support drew level with them, just before the *Green Tree* pub, *The Family* started a song. It wasn't the type of song that was associated with a battle cry but that's what it was. They'd seen their team well beaten, it was pissing down with rain and now they were being mocked by their hated rivals. Given this mood, it wasn't the song you'd associate with such disappointment.

"Raindrops are falling on my head
And just like the guy whose feet
Are too big for his bed
Nothing seems to fit
Those raindrops
Are falling on my head
They keep falling"

The Jambos on the other side of Gorgie Road, streaming out of the game, didn't know how to react. *The Family* did. As the last breath of the vocal came out, they attacked. They had lain among the scarfers until they spotted the Hearts mob appearing and they steamed into them like an express train heading out of Haymarket station on the tunnel above them. Punches and kicks landed a more accurately than shots on goal from the Hibs team, a few folk were headbutted out the game and when all was said and done, the Hearts mob, plus a few plucky fans, had been battered. One particularly unlucky Hearts casual had been floored coming out between two cars, ready to rumble, then floored by one punch from Luke Doyle. A younger Hibs fan, not part of the casuals, attempted to jumped on the prostrate Jambo but was pulled back by John Quinlivan.

By the time the police were on the scene in numbers, *The Family* were long gone up towards Fountainbridge whilst some of the Hearts contingent decanted to the *Red Oak* pub to lick their wounds and dull the pain of the severe bleaching they had just taken whilst other fans, who happened to just be in the wrong place at the wrong time, were heading home with

a sair face wondering where that had
been on their list of new year resolutions.

'Whores of the Empire'

Sandy C. was the keyholder. Nobody got in the building until he arrived. It was quiet around Leith that day. The 2nd of January was a holiday in Scotland designed to prove that Scots could drink more than the English, but Leith had a severe hangover. The start of a new decade coupled with their team's pitiful performance at Tynecastle had made most of Leith turn back over when their alarm clocks had gone off this morning.

Not so in Joppa.

Vicky had woken Sandy C. with a cup of tea and a promise that his breakfast was on the table but, on arrival via the dark blue carpet and matching cream-coloured doors of bedroom and living room, Sandy's eyes lit up. There was no breakfast on table although it had clearly been cooked judging by the smells of bacon and sausage wafting in from the kitchen. There was even a hint of egg, but Sandy C. couldn't quite decipher if it was poached, fried or scrambled. Partly because the main thrust of his focus was on the plastic mat that was laid out neatly on the living room floor carpet.

"Really?"

Sandy C. asked in the way an excited child would when pointed in the direction of an open sweetie cupboard at their Nana's.

Vicky nodded.

Vicky knew her man well and although she gained little sexual gratification from the practice, she took solace in the fact that Sandy C. still took pleasure in looking at her gaping vagina. She had been paranoid about it for a while. In her teens, she had been caressed there a few times by boys who usually had an odour of *Brut* and *El Dorado*. One, in a lane just off Restalrig Road South, even licked his fingers after touching her and this made her recoil internally but later made her touch herself. She remembered the incident a lot after Sandy C. had climaxed and she still needed to. The boy, Stevie Wright his name was, had a *Mickey Mouse* watch on that he had told her that his Ma had bought him at Ingliston Market. That meant every time Vicky had cause to pass there, the bizarre statue of *King Kong* and all, she remembered a boy licking her pussy juice off his fingers as the hands of Mickey went back and forth.

The paranoia regarding her gash started on June 2nd, 1983. She had been at work, manager of the *Jacket Boot* pub in Spittal Street, a boozer frequented by lots of Edinburgh polis and therefore a hotbed of Masons, plus also handy for Sandy C.'s work in nearby High Riggs.

The staff had been working hard after a harsh winter and, occasionally, a couple stayed in the pub overnight so that it would be open the next day for the punters despite the dreadful snow that had engulfed Edinburgh in the winter of 1982. (Sandy C. had said that it was God punishing the Catholics for coming out in their thousands to see Pope John Paul II speak at Murrayfield. Sandy C. had been a tacit follower of the Scotland rugby team up until Murrayfield announced they would host the visit. Vicky got his logic up to a point, but she felt punished as she trudged through the snow to dig out the car every morning and as a proud member of the lodge and The Eastern Star, she hated Catholics as much as anyone. It had shaken Scotland's defenders of the Protestant faith to the core though. Thousands of Catholic school children had had been transported into the capital. There had been protests at various entry points to Edinburgh and stones had been thrown at buses in Haymarket. The actual mass itself, organised in Scotland by James Bonner, head of communications for the Catholic Church in Scotland, had been a massive success. Nuns acted as stewards and when the Holy Father came into the stadium the crowd sang "John Paul reigns" over and over again followed by the Rodgers and Hammerstein ballad *You'll Never Walk Alone* which infuriated the likes of Sandy C. because of its connections to Celtic and the fact they had just won the league again. He could handle many things but gloating Fenians was, even for a man who had walked all over Scotland and the north of Ireland, a step too far. It was discussed by the higher echelons of the LOL in Scotland and, eventually dismissed. The consensus being that whilst the visit had been a dark week for Scotland, the Orange Order remained strong with over 50,000 members whereas the Catholics would soon fade away again albeit with a less then gentle shove from the Order)

A staff night out had been arranged and a local cinema worker had dropped off tickets for Vicky and staff as a thank you for all their hard work. They decided to make a night of it after one of the younger barmaids, Lizzie (Claim to fame: Shagged in the flat upstairs by a chief inspector who she said had a 12 inch cock that hadn't been up his wife this side of the silver jubilee) suggested they go to *The Bass Rock* bar round the corner first as "the sounds were good" (Reality being she had actually taken one up the bum in the toilets from a 43 year old *Sigue Sigue Sputnik* fan from Bristol the week before and fancied bumping into him again as she swore he had said, when chatting her up, he was in Edinburgh for a fortnight on business) Lizzie herself was 54 but dressed like a 23 year old. She could be that specific because, on nights out and shifts in the bar, she often wore her own daughter's clothes. She had worked in *Nipples*, the strip bar in Bread Street in the days before her tits didn't sag like *Droopy's* ears and was grateful when Vicky gave her a job in the *Boot* after a short interview. Both her sexual prowess and appetite were the stuff of legend. One day she had given a local copper a hand job in a room in the back of the strip bar and the bobby let it be known to anyone who would listen that she had made him cum quicker than Nanette Newman film appearances had done in his youth. (He particularly recalled going to the *Dominion* and watching *Séance on a Wet Afternoon* where she played the wife of the guy who went on to play Alan Bradley in *Coronation Street*)

All the cops loved Lizzie.

Indeed, the chief inspector story, about Roderick Puncheon, had also become the stuff of legend. He had been working on the disappearance of two girls, teenagers, from a pub in the Royal Mile of Edinburgh, *The Jupiter Start*, and the case was going nowhere. He had started hitting the drink hard and his wife even harder. They lived in the plush Marchmont area of Edinburgh and had a reasonably happy if unspectacular marriage. His wife, Susanna, was a pillar of the community type who helped with the local church and Rotary Club in equal measure, they'd married in 1970 after a brief courtship but hadn't had any kids. Indeed, they had barely had sex in years. Susanna had always complained that Roderick's cock had hurt her and so, little by little, sex was off the menu and pork pies and sausage rolls were on it as jumble sales took precedent over Roddy's Jumbo Cock.

This had been burning away at Roddy. He threw himself into work and the case of the two missing girls seemed the ideal distraction from the lack of bedroom activity. Yet, like the bedroom, it went nowhere and began to become a noose round his neck. He had gone home one evening and had snapped. Susanna looked pathetic to him, like John Lennon's Auntie Mimi without the fire, and he slapped her across the face after she had asked him if he had wanted rice pudding (from a tin) for dessert. He then stormed out and went to the *Jacket Boot* for solace and strong whiskey. He had gone in and saw Lizzie behind the bar.

Inside he was burning. He knew all about Lizzie's reputation and he wanted to show her who was boss. His wife and work couldn't provide that self-esteem so Lizzie would have to. Lizzie, as per the rules, knew never to throw out a polis until they were finished drinking and she had kept a close eye on Chief Inspector Puncheon as he propped up the bar. He had no real patter so just went for it, the words manoeuvring their way past the *Glenfiddoch* still lingering on his taste buds…

"Fancy a fuck?"

The words stopped Lizzie in her tracks for a second. Only a second, mind. Her response was akin to stripping off, bending over and opening wide even if it only consisted of two words.

"Well now"

Despite his limited experience in this department, Roddy knew he was in.

After emptying the till and shutting down the lights, Lizzie led the top cop upstairs. It was a small flight, but Roddy could already feel the need to unleash the beast. His frustrations of a frigid wife and cold case had been eating him alive and he needed to burst out and remind everyone who was boss. Lizzie entered the small flat, flicked a switch under the tall lampshade and turned to face Roddy.

"Fancy a drink?"

He didn't. Instead, he approached her like a lion approaching a barely alive deer and ripped her shirt open, exposing her black bra that contained her more than ample bosom. Roddy grabbed Lizzie's breasts with such ferocity even a vastly experienced sexual queen like her was heard to say:

"Easy Tiger"

But the chief wouldn't be stopped. After ripping her bra off in the same way a 5 year old dismantles a chocolate wrapper, Lizzie was in about Roddy's belt and taking down his M&S trousers and pants to reveal the monster in front her. Only semi-hard yet still spectacular, the sight caused Lizzie to utter:

"Fucking hell, has some cunt been hinging fae that?"

Years of sexual inactivity and incompetence at work had brought Chief Inspector Roderick Puncheon to this point. Yet it was a matter of hours of Lizzie telling the story that saw Roddy earn a new nickname: Puncheon the Truncheon.

None of which explains Vicky's paranoia. They had their drinks in the *Bass Rock* and daundered along to the *ABC* on Lothian Road for the last showing of *Return of the Jedi*. All girls and all pissed, there was much hilarity getting in and touching up a young, male, Usher who seemed bemused. They took their seats and, once the noise settled down, were transfixed by the screen. Mainly because the adverts were all for local businesses and the *Jacket Boot* wasn't one of them. They sang along to the *Pearl and Dean* music as a few voices around them told them to "shut up"

As the film started, most of the ladies fell asleep. Vicky didn't though. She became immersed in the spectacular special effects on screen and the unfolding 'good versus evil' story unfolding before her eyes. She even started to side with Luke Skywalker despite his anti-establishment stance and refusal to castigate prisoners. She felt pangs of dread as imperial-like guards pushed Skywalker along a plank towards his inevitable death in the *Sarlaac Pit*. At the point it looked like he would be damned to it, a screech was heard by Vicky. The sort of screech that would make your blood run cold. The sort of screech that would awaken the demons in hell. The sort of screech that would make you run for more than the ice cream van…

"THAT LOOKS LIKE AN AULD WUMMIN'S BLART!!!!"

It was from one of her entourage, but it was still the night that Vicky's vaginal paranoia was born.

'Beware of the risen people'

John was rough but ok. He had a lie in and then a bath that cleared most of the hangover but swallowed three *Disprin* with water just to be on safe side. He had letters to post and was briskly walking to the post box outside *Frasiers* before popping in for a cure. The letters were to alert the members there was a meeting this Friday of the Connolly crew. He had meant to get them away last week, but time got the better of him. He would do a phone round tomorrow night, but the letters were a good back up as well. After posting all and taking a lingering look up and down the road, he walked in the pub. The High Street itself was vastly different from Hogmanay. Aside from a few road sweepers, the odd tourist struggling with a map and a car now and then, the place was pretty empty.

As indeed the pub was.

There were a few in, it was still a holiday, but all but one of the tables were unoccupied and there were three guys and one couple there, all drinking. John marched in, a copy of *The Guardian* under his arm, and recognised one of the men at the bar, Billy, a non-confrontational Rangers supporter who was asking Tam the barman about getting the Celtic v Rangers game on the radio. John nodded at him and saw that Billy looked a bit out of sorts. They shook hands, wished each other 'Happy New Year' and Billy went back to being a bit perplexed.

"What's the matter Billy, the game's no even started yet"

Billy shook his head.

"You ken me John, am no a bigot, ah talk to you and yer boys, nae sweat"
John was now a bit perplexed. What the fuck was this cunt on about?

"If ma daughter walked in the hoose wi a Catholic, it widnae bother me. Ah wisnae one of them at Ibrox burning ma scarf when Mo Johnston signed, ah hink he's a fucking great player"

John was now even more bemused.

Before he could interject, Billy kept going.
"New Year's Day, well morning ken, half one, quarter tae two, the door goes. I thought it wid be big Harvey eh? He's normally my first fit. Anyway, the wife opens it and in marches the daughter dragging some fucking Coon boy wi her"

At that point John clicked like a seat belt.

Tam had put a pint of lager in front of John and they exchanged glances in an "Aye, I know" kind of way.

John considered remonstrating with Billy but couldn't be arsed. It wasn't that he didn't care, he very much did so, but people like Billy were collateral damage who would either fall in line or be taken the fuck out, come the revolution.

The revolution though, for now, could wait.

John started to feel a bit rough again so took a seat and unrolled his paper for a quiet read with his pint. He had hit the bevvy hard over the Christmas and New Year period (Technically he was still in it) and, to add insult to injury, had chipped a tooth whilst have a lunch of meat and tatties with his auld man earlier in the day before his auld man drove through to the fitba. Unlike John, his auld man James was a massive Celtic supporter and would right now be taking his place in the mass of Fenians currently congregating in *The Jungle*. Seany Beef would be there as well if he had left the boozer yet that is. Whilst James Gerard Quinlivan was your 'I'll slit your fucking throat if you even think about badmouthing Celtic' type of Tim, Seany

Beef was more of a pragmatist. He'd chin you for having a go but would admit to himself you were probably right as he lay on his couch the morning after. Seany was always at John's side. Known all over Edinburgh as an Irish Republican, his casual demeanour could often be mistaken for weakness or even stupidity, but Seany Beef was neither weak nor stupid. For all his legendary humour (He had a magnificent talent for giving people nicknames that always stuck) he was a committed and dedicated Republican who had respect all over Scotland and Ireland. In those kinds of circles, that means a lot. You better fucking believe it does. John and Seany were young guys who were trying to change the world in the face of a multitude of opposition that loved to combine hate with being stubborn and pig-headed ignorance rolled up an in a parcel of threats and attempted intimidation. (Note the word "attempted" in that last sentence) These guys didn't roll over for anyone, knew anyone who was anyone in Edinburgh and had the backing of an army based predominantly in the north of Ireland.

John had become so engrossed in his thoughts he hadn't realised that the Celtic-Rangers game was now blasting out of a decent sixed radio at the close end of the bar. It sounded like Rangers were on top and, inevitably, scored through Nigel Spackman.

"Ya fucking beauty!!!"

Cried Billy, now awoken from his sardonic slumber.

John was emotionless. He had liked Celtic as a kid but was drawn towards Hibs because of friends and fighting. He still wanted Celtic to win but nowhere near as much as his auld man, or Seany Beef for that matter, would. He didn't like to see Huns celebrating though, especially racist prick ones like Billy.

"Sounds like Mark Walters is having a good game, Billy, some player he is"

Billy looked at John sheepishly.

"Aye, eh, good player aye"

John knew he had him.

"Some would say the best in Scotland. That shimmy he does is different class eh?"

Billy felt as though lava was spewing through his body. He knew he had to change the subject.

"Imagine a cunt called Nigel scoring in an Old Firm game eh? Oan a Scottish holiday as well"

Billy smiled he was sure he had got out of that particular bear trap.

John also smiled, the radio in the background crackled away with commentary from the game, one of the few instances he could remember when a full game was being heard on the radio. John did like the radio. The political stuff mainly but the fitba stuff too. He didn't get to every Hibs game, so Radio Scotland was his main source of information when not there. He wasn't one for magazines like *Shoot* or *Match* and this new 'Club Call' phenomenon that was springing up he found absolutely ludicrous (Fans were asked to phone a premium rate number in order to find out the latest 'exclusives' from their clubs)

"The Celtic defence should have sent for *XTC* eh?"

John quipped and it completely flummoxed Billy.

"No mind the song Billy? *'We're only making plans, for NIGEL!'*

Billy did but remained in an uneasy feeling. John continued…

"Great song that, about the bullied. Folk who would like to put certain people in categories, *know your place* and all that. Taking out their own insecurities on those they perceive to be beneath them but, in reality, (John begun to whisper), it will be them who take over the world, eh Billy?"

Billy was now in state of flux. He had only one way out.

"You fancy another pint, John?"

John grinned.

"No, I'm fine Billy, you horse on yourself though"

John turned the page on his newspaper.

'Whores of the Empire'

This was the elite. There was the masonic lodge then the orange lodge and then the *Black*. Rarely visible, these were the men who controlled every facet of Loyalism in Edinburgh. Whether you wanted to march or fight in the streets, you had to go through these men. It had been easy for a long time. Aside from a few real hard men out of the likes of Niddry, Gilmerton, Leith and Pilton, there had been little challenge to their supremacy in the east. Glasgow was a different kettle of fish with weight of numbers guaranteeing authority. Edinburgh was a different game altogether. There hadn't been any catholic ghettos, outside of the so-called *'Little Ireland'* in the Cowgate where friends on the council ensured that a homeless shelter would open therefore devaluing properties. Then there was the advent of late licences and night clubs that ensured sleep was a distant memory for those who still bode in the area. It was just bitterness laced with a sadistic sense of humour that fuelled these things. There was no evidence to suggest that there was a bigger than average Irish or Catholic population living in the area since the 1960's. It didn't matter to these men, in this hut, with this amount of power. They were representatives of the *Royal Black Institution* and that stood for something.

Especially this year.

"Gentleman, first let us toast *Her Majesty the Queen* and then me let me wish each of you a happy and healthy new year in this glorious of years, the 300th anniversary of King William the Third's victory over the rebel forces in the Battle of the Boyne"

Brother Kenneth Hewitt always did the honours.

Sandy C. one of five other men in the room, seated around a black velvet table, listening thought of Vicky and her paranoia.

The others around the table were hard line Loyalists from varying backgrounds. Kenneth had worked in the civil service for 46 years, 34 as a manager before his retirement whereas Donald Watson was a member of Edinburgh City Council. Davie Robb was a foreman with McAlpine's, Alan Phillips was a lawyer who did all the *Black* legal work whereas Jimmy McGregor worked for the DHSS as a sniffer for longer than he could remember, sharing an office with Sandy C.

Sandy C. had been a sniffer of note for many years. Based in High Riggs, a few goosesteps from the *Jacket Boot*, he had a nose for a certain type of 'client' that walked through the door of the brew each day. The unsuspecting victim would walk in, look at a few jobs, write down the ones they were interested in, join the queue to sign on and then, on arrival at the desk and picking up the pen in anticipation of doing the damage, they would be told that the investigations department wanted a word, and they should take a seat until called. The soft porn equivalent of being told you had a terminal disease, but you'd need to wait over there until we can tell you when it will kill you. Then you'd called in by either Sandy C. or Jimmy McGregor (they took it in turns) but you could bet your bottom fiver that both would be grilling you.

Those who worked on the front line of the brew had noticed the pattern. It was one of those unsaid things for two reasons. The first being that those who noticed the pattern didn't know the significance and the other, far more in the minority, did know and were too scared to say anything. One guy noticed and wasn't scared to mention it. Not to his manager or even *the* manager. Not to his work mates or even his mates at work.

No. He did tell John Patrick Quinlivan though.

"Sandy C. and his cohort McGregor only ever seem to pull in people with Irish, Catholic names or with Asian backgrounds" Tony Galente told John over the phone one night. Galente, who had started working on the front line of the brew three months, was lower profile among the Connolly boys but a Connolly boy all the same. He was on good terms with Sandy C. and Jimmy. They had been introduced as "The two Jambos" by a tall, baldy guy with John Lennon style glasses called Paul who was Hibs daft and had worked in High Riggs for 12 years. They once asked what team Tony supported, and he declared "Scotland" so shared football banter often, Jimmy being the more affable of the two. Tony never spoke about politics or religion, so they just took it that Tony's Ma had a good time in Italy once.

Tony would ask them about various Hearts-related stuff, and they'd talk Scotland with him, assuming him to be a fan, as he dropped in bits and pieces about the forthcoming World Cup in Italy. It was Scotland's fifth World Cup in a row, but all were unsure about the management team.

"Roxburgh and Brown? Pair of fucking school teachers" espoused Sandy C.

"Wee Craigie is awright" pinged back Jimmy.

That opinion was not based on his football coaching ability, more that Jimmy remembered that Craig Brown was a Brother.

Tony speculated on the potential inclusion of John Collins in the squad as he had been having a great season at Easter Road which caused Sandy C. and Jimmy to raise eyebrows with perfect synergy.

"Collins? The wee Pape from Hibs? Na, no chance. I'd take Davie Cooper still"

Sandy C. was Hearts through and through but loved Davie Cooper of Rangers. Cooper had reportedly been booted out of Ibrox after not taking too kindly to Rangers breaking their policy of apartheid with the signing of the Roman Catholic, and former Celtic player, Maurice Johnston. He was often heard remarking that Cooper would have flourished in a better team with a left foot like his.

"He would have flourished in a better team with a left foot like his"

Sandy C. remarked.

Tony felt like pushing it just a little.

"Collins has got no a bad left foot as well"

Both Sandy C. and Jimmy smiled and shook their heads.

Tony would leave their cubby hole of an office and think to himself:

"What a pair of cunts"

Back among the *Black*, there were bigger fish to fry.

Davie Robb spoke

"Ok, we need to talk vermin and extermination. You'll all be aware of the rise of this fucking *Connolly* thing that, despite our best efforts, continues to be a baw ache. Now, we have gone down the traditional routes of threats and intimidation. We ensured they couldn't get office space in Edinburgh, but they managed to get an Edinburgh P.O. Box that's actually based in Prestonpans. We lobbied the council using Donald here's connections but those two Fenian pricks on the council fae Niddry and Craigmillar put a block on it. So, we need to stop fucking about here and get serious"

"How serious?"

Alan was curious.

"Deadly serious"

Came back Davie.

"As far as I am concerned, we need to draw a fucking line in the sand here. We've got these cunts infesting our city centre every year, we've got they sell oot cunts in South Africa talking aboot releasing that terrorist Mandela and we've got RANGERS SIGNING A FUCKING CATHOLIC!!!"

The last part made the Hearts supporting Sandy C. and Jimmy chortle. They knew how much Davie loved his Rangers and how broken he had been when the blonde taig had pitched up in a Rangers tie. The exact same type of Rangers tie Davie reserved for social occasions that didn't require fill masonic or orange regalia.

Davie hadn't worn that tie at any time after July 10th, 1989.

The anger was palpable among the Rangers support after that day. After 20 odd years in the doldrums (aside from a couple flare ups in the mid-late 70's) Graeme Souness came in as Player/Manager had started to get to the peak of Scottish football with the signing of some top, quality English internationals like Terry Butcher and Chris Woods. Graham Roberts had endeared himself by conducting 40,000 singing *The Sash* at Ibrox whilst Richard Gough was the kind of Swedish born-South African-WASP-Scottish guy that was always welcome at Ibrox. That was all fine. As was the signing of the Jewish Avi Cohen and black Mark Walters (the latter endearing himself by regularly tearing Celtic apart) But signing a Catholic? And no just any Catholic, but him? Fucking Johnston. The prick that had the audacity to bless himself against Rangers? in a cup final?

Who the fuck did he think he was?

Davie would often remark to anyone who would listen that:

"The wee prick hated us that much he never even scored at Parkheid against us, jist Ibrox"

Johnston scoring the winner v Celtic at Ibrox and Rangers winning yesterday at Celtic Park had done nothing to calm Davie's mood.

It ran deep with Davie. Which is why, at this meeting of the *Black*, he said the following words:

"I've spoken to people in Belfast and Portadown. They want to send a guy over to sort this out once and for all"

Furrowed brows went round the hut like a Mexican wave.

Kenneth was the first to break the silence:

"What exactly do you mean, Davie"

Davie pulled up a folder from under the table, opened it, took out a photo and then flipped it over onto the table.

"John Quinlivan, that's what I mean. This cunt needs sorted for good"

'Beware of the risen people'

Seany Beef was on the couch. He had managed to put a shift in today but was, as the Aussies say, "pushing through". His Ma and Dad were out at an Aunties. He had the house in Leith to himself. Now was the time for rest, relaxation and contemplation. He had taped a few things over Christmas and now had the chance to watch them whilst munching on some much needed *Quality Street* left over from Christmas. (He had an egg roll for breakfast yesterday and nothing since- The boys had something in *Sinnita's Café* this morning, he ordered a cup of a tea and a *Mars* bar. He couldn't even face the chocolate)

The day previous, he gone on the Leith bus that ran out of *The Big Wheel* pub on Ferry Road. Seany wasn't a huge drinker but occasionally had a huge drink and the day before had been one of those occasions. The game had been awful. Celtic, dreadful for most of the season, had been as threatening as a balloon on a stick and once Rangers scored, through NIGEL fucking Spackman for Christ sake, they never looked like losing their lead. That was infuriating thing for Seany, Rangers didn't have to be that good but were still miles better. After the game and back on the bus, he had a couple in *The Big Wheel* then ended up in *Toby's* on Leith Walk that ended in a major session when a guy he knew from Donegal came in about 10 minutes before Brenny, Seany's big brother, who had listened to the game on the radio, had appeared and before they could say "Party" 50 bottles of *Becks* had been sought from the bar, on a promise they would be replaced in the morning and they ended up back at the guy from Donegal's flat in Buchanan Street. He could never remember the guy's name. He had staggered in at 4.32am and was up again for work at 7.15am when the digital clock alarm penetrated his ears like the four-minute warning. A day scooting about in the work's van going from job to job had Seany ready for a night on the couch.

Then he heard some noise that door.

At first, he thought he was hearing things.

It was a familiar noise that he was well used to but not at this time of night. Not when he was stretched out on the couch enjoying some well-earned, in his mind, rest. The noise was confirmed when two young faces burst through the living room door, both holding a carton of *Kia Ora* with a straw sticking out. They were followed by an even bigger, much more familiar figure. Brenny. Seany's big brother Brendan Beef, Brenny to everyone except his mother.
Brenny appeared with the kids in tow on the lookout for a favour.

From Seany.

"Alright? Ma said you were daeing nout, could you watch the bairns for a couple of hours? Til Ma and Dad come back. Angela (Brenny's wife) and I are going out for a meal with her parents. Ma said they could both sleep in the spare room, alright?"

Seany noticed the question was rhetorical.

Brenny was Seany's older brother by two years. He loved him but also thought he could be a pain in the arse at times. He had a knack of always assuming that the world stopped when he needed something for him or his family. As far as Seany's nephews were concerned, that was right, Seany doted on them. Just not after a hard day's graft with a hangover.

"Are they ready for their bed now?"

Seany said more in hope than expectation as he rose from the couch, swinging his legs round to land between the couch and coffee table.

"Naw. Thing is, Ma and Dad were roond before they went to Auntie Kathleen's and they filled the bairns with chocolate, so they are hyper"

Even my Ma and Dad hate me thought Seany.

Seany got the boys down by 9.43pm. It was an arduous task given that they used his couch as trampoline for most of the evening and liberated all the diluting juice in the house as well after finishing their *Kia Ora* in double quick time.

Seany's arse was just about to be back on the couch when the phone went. He moved as fast as he had all day and grabbed the receiver after two rings, worried that it would awaken the dynamic duo now out for the count in the spare room.

It was the familiar voice of John Quinlivan.

They chatted about the fitba and respective hangovers before John got to the point of the call.

"The back room of the *Northender* is booked, and I sent a mail out yesterday and did a ring round the night. Most of the boys got the letter before they went to work"

Seany craned his neck in the lobby and saw that there was a letter for him on the wee table next to the front door above where the family kept their shoes. He hadn't noticed it before, and no one had alerted him to the fact that it was there. He marvelled at the postal service in his mind and thought about how happy he was that bastard Thatcher hadn't managed to get her claws into the *Royal Mail.* Cunts had to be good for something he thought.

They ended the call with "See you on Friday" and "Aye"

Seany put the receiver down and walked back thinking:

"At last, some peace and quiet"

It was only when entering then living room again that he noticed the two empty *Kia Ora* cartons and the fact that the bairns had spilt all the contents on the couch.

'Whores of the Empire'

Sandy C. made his way into work from the East Fountainbridge entrance. Moving upstairs gingerly, he bypassed the staff room as usual and got to the office he shared with Jimmy to find him already on tea duty. They had a routine they stuck to. One came in early one day to do the tea then the roles reversed the following day. The office opened at 8.30am (except on Fridays when it was 9am) on the dot but neither Sandy C. nor Jimmy felt any need for urgency at this time in the morning. Their drill was the same most days, they had picked out the files the day before of those they wanted a quiet word with then sat back the next day and waited for their victims to voluntarily flood in from various parts of the city, completely unaware of what lay in store for them on arrival.

The official party line was that these people were under investigation for suspected offences relating to benefit fraud. A lot of this was reliant on information received from an anonymous tip line that either received or recorded messages from various grasses of the general public. The posters were all over the city on walls and in bus shelters.

'Shop the Stealers-Call 031 229 1874'

Indeed, the general public still bought the line that when they signed off after getting a job, their file was then destroyed. This was untrue. In the depths of High Riggs job centre was a place that staff members called *Dormant.* In *Dormant* were filing cabinets. Lots and lots of filing cabinets, all filled with inactive details of anyone who had ever set foot in High Riggs, whether they were now working, emigrated or even deceased. This was not allowed but no one challenged it.

The reality of investigation was also somewhat different for Jimmy and Sandy C.

Their agenda often relied on the same kind of tip offs but none of them were anonymous. Information would come from various members of both lodges, various friends and associates of a loyalist persuasion and several people who liked to support Hearts.

The goal was clear. To suppress and marginalise as many Irish Catholics and those of an Asian background in the Edinburgh area.

Or, as Sandy C. put it:

"Making sure the Taigs and Pakis know their fucking place"

That was it. That's what it was all about. All the meetings and marching. The sashes and secrets. The bowler hats and brown brogues. They were all components of a Protestant supremacy that people like Sandy C. cherished. It wasn't enough to prosper, the enemy must be kept down as well. In their place.

He knew what kind the likes of Quinlivan and Beef were, riff-raff. Low rent thugs who couldn't shine his shoes. Them? A threat? He thought the idea of bringing someone over to sort out Quinlivan was wrong. All wrong. They could handle him in Edinburgh. Sandy had told Jimmy as much after the meeting of the *Black*.

Sandy C. had encountered Quinlivan a few times. He had his usual vantage point at the toilets at the east end of the Meadows where the Connolly march ended, mainly to check out numbers and he had noted that they were rising. He had also met him in the street twice, once in the Lawnmarket where they had a brief chat and once on Leith Walk where Sandy C. had been waiting on a bus outside the Masonic Club. Neither had given much away although Sandy C. had noted how non-plussed Quinlivan had seemed. That had unnerved Sandy C. because he expected his type to be volatile and brash. Quinlivan was more affable and unconcerned. The more Sandy C. thought about that, the more confused he got. Was he softening or was John Quinlivan genuinely not bothered about him, his organisations and their grip on the city of Edinburgh?

Sandy C. had contemplated that and put it down to a mixture of naivety and youthful ignorance. This was their city. John Cormack and *Protestant Action* had rubber-stamped that in the 30's when they got nine councillors elected with 31% of the vote. At its peak, *Protestant Action* had 8000 members and could mobilise numbers of more than 20,000 like it did when the *Eucharistic Congress*, a gathering of various Roman Catholic clergy, were jeered and attacked in the infamous *Morningside Riot* of June 1935

It was tales of *that* Edinburgh that Sandy C. had been brought up on by his father, Alexander C. and his uncle, Walter F. They had both been part of *Protestant*

Action until there were problems with the Orange Order (Cormack had wanted an amalgamation between the *Order* and the *Action* but, after lots of wrangling, it didn't happen, and Cormack left in 1939)

Sandy C. remembered his father and uncle telling these stories on Hogmanay where they would all partake in a whiskey. It was one of the few times that his elders would partake. Neither celebrated Christmas. Before the Reformation in 1560, Christmas in Scotland had been a religious feasting day. Then, with the powerful Kirk frowning upon anything related to Roman Catholicism, the Scottish Parliament passed a law in 1640 that made celebrating 'Yule vacations' illegal. Even after Charles II was restored to the throne, celebrating Christmas was frowned upon in Scotland for a long time – it wasn't until 1958 that 25 December became a Scottish public holiday.

Being traditionalists, Alexander C. and Walter F. saw Christmas as part of a Papal conspiracy designed to make Protestants spend their money on frivolous things like presents for family and toys for kids. For long, long time periods, both Alexander C. and Walter F. would lecture a grateful young Sandy C. on the perils of owning such things as a Hula Hoop or Pogo Stick. Instead, young Sandy C. would delight in being told stories from his elders about how their struggle to keep Protestant supremacy supreme in Edinburgh was real and that Roman Catholics didn't ruin Protestant lives with their doctrines and dogma. One of the things that really grinded the gears of the brothers was the Roman Catholic Church in its formula of baptism still asking that the parents and godparents of infants that are to be baptised recite the Apostles' Creed as a sign that they accept the basic doctrines of the church and will help their children grow in the Catholic faith. Indeed, this had become a point of angst for Sandy C.

later in life. He had had been addressing an Orange march in Prestonpans in 1981 and there had been a gathering of local youths, Celtic supporters, Fenians, who had attempted to disrupt his speech. As Sandy C. was pouring his usual scorn on the Catholic Church and their insistence on the recital of the Apostles' Creed as an acceptance of the doctrines in the Catholic faith. As he was bringing his tone to Paisley-like levels when one of the youths shouted-"whit, him fae the Rocky films?"

'Beware of the risen people'

John had stepped in on his auld man. It was part new year greeting visit, part necessity of a procuring of funds to set him up for the meeting tomorrow. His auld man greeted him warmly enough at the door but could feel the bite coming from 500 yards.

"Want a cup ae tea?"

John nodded and planted himself on the one chair that accompanied the couch. It was a tenement block and James had a one bedroom flat within that. The couch doubled as a bed and was ideal for John when he needed a doss in the city centre for one reason or another. Although to James and John, it would always be the southside.

Question Time was on tonight as well. John had forgot to tape it. Upon mentioning this to his auld man, his reply was so quick that he would make a great contestant on *Going for Gold*.

"I'll get the blankets and spare pillow from the cupboard"

John then cast his line.

"Could you spare me a score until January 20th when the bursary comes in?"

James thought for a second, a quick calculation let him know that John would now owe him £380 on January 20th, assuming this was his last tap before then.

'Whores of the Empire'

Sandy C. rattled the change in is pocket as he entered the phone box. The door took its customary age to shut but he waited until it did before picking up the receiver. He had a quick look behind him before dialling the number he long since had memorised.

"Davie? Aye. Tonight, ok, see you there"

The aroma of pish was now noticeable in his nostrils.

He stepped out of the phone box and looked down at the *Jacket Boot*. He thought about a quick dram but knew he didn't have the time. He headed towards it anyway and entered like a man who had just staggered in from the Sahara Desert. He saw Vicky changing and optic behind the bar and she saw him in the McEwan's mirror. She turned and looked him straight in the eye as he spoke.

"I'll not be in until late tonight, darling"

She nodded and watched Sandy C. about turn and go back out the same door he came in, with the picture of *King Billy* above it.

'Beware of the risen people'

There were a few members in already by the time John and Seany appeared. They always liked to meet five minutes before entering the pub or Seany would pick John up in the work's van and they'd discuss anything they needed to before the meeting.

The pub was ideal. At the north end of Edinburgh's southside, it was easily accessible for guys coming from Niddry, Gilmerton, Muirhouse and Leith with buses from all these places headed in that direction, frequently. That was important because all members were working class and lived week to week. Occasionally there would be some plummy mouthed intellectual type who would appear and would want to philosophise the politics of Irish freedom and there would always be plenty banter around them but often they would drift away when they realised that this organisation was more than a talking shop with occasional leaflet drop.

One who had stayed the course though was Henry Charles.

He stood right away because he was a bit older than the average Connolly member and had an air of a *middle-class do-gooder* about him (Especially with a name like *Henry Charles*-although a common theme of council schemes was that anyone called *Henry* was almost always a fucking headcase and *Henry Charles* certainly wasn't one of them) but there was more to him than that and he, through time, gained the respect of all involved and was happy to join in the banter. Which was handy given the one thing about him that no one else among the Connolly boys had in common with him:

He was a Hearts supporter.

A few of the boys had a minor issue with that but by and large, it tickled most of them and provided ample content for banter. It didn't really matter of course, and John had always said this was never about football (although there were occasions when he had a lager or two that he would extol the virtues of James Connolly being a Hibby. Something a few members always disputed for the craic) but a lot of the boys had got to Republican politics via the fitba. A lot of the boys had been brought up with *The Wolfe Tones* tapes on buses and had heard the same songs in *The Jungle* at Celtic Park and away grounds all over Scotland.

Through those, it started to peak their interest in politics and maybe they started to buy the odd book that enhanced their political education. *The Provisional IRA* by Patrick Bishop and Eamonn Mallie had been popular (not least for the panic it created when pulled out on a bus going through an Edinburgh scheme) as had *The Workers Republic* which contained selected writings from James Connolly himself and, of course, *The Ragged Trousered Philanthropists* by Robert

Tressell which had changed the lives of many young men in the past.

Of course, within the Connolly organisation there was plenty political discussion. The was a direct consequence of various initiatives designed to support Republican prisoners held captive in jails all over England and Ireland. As well as fundraising, there were book drives to gain the type of books that were always popular among Republican prisoners. Books on those engaged in their own struggle in various parts of history. People like Fidel Castro, Che Guevara, Nelson Mandela and Steve Biko always grabbed the attention. Quickly, they became the reading material of the Connolly boys and there had been a copy of *Borstal Boy* by Brendan Behan circulating around various houses of activists in Edinburgh for a while which had initially been owned by Seany Beef.

Something that Connolly had written way back in 1899 had struck a chord with the boys now and it become the backbone of which the organisation relied on.

Let us free Ireland! Never mind such base, carnal thoughts as concern work and wages, healthy homes, or lives unclouded by poverty.

Let us free Ireland! The rackrenting landlord; is he not also an Irishman, and wherefore should we hate him? Nay, let us not speak harshly of our brother – yea, even when he raises our rent.

Let us free Ireland! The profit-grinding capitalist, who robs us of three-fourths of the fruits of our labour, who sucks the very marrow of our bones when we are young, and then throws us out in the street, like a worn-out tool when we are grown prematurely old in his service, is he not an Irishman, and mayhap a patriot, and wherefore should we think harshly of him?

Let us free Ireland! "The land that bred and bore us." And the landlord who makes us pay for permission to live upon it. Whoop it up for liberty!

"Let us free Ireland," says the patriot who won't touch Socialism. Let us all join together and cr-r-rush the br-r-rutal Saxon. Let us all join together, says he, all classes and creeds. And, says the town worker, after we have crushed the Saxon and freed Ireland, what will we do? Oh, then you can go back to your slums, same as before. Whoop it up for liberty!

And, says the agricultural workers, after we have freed Ireland, what then? Oh, then you can go scraping around for the landlord's rent or the money-lenders' interest same as before. Whoop it up for liberty!

After Ireland is free, says the patriot who won't touch socialism, we will protect all classes, and if you won't pay your rent you will be evicted same as now. But the evicting party, under command of the sheriff, will wear green uniforms and the Harp without the Crown, and the warrant turning you out on the roadside will be stamped with the arms of the Irish Republic. Now, isn't that worth fighting for?

And when you cannot find employment, and, giving up the struggle of life in despair, enter the poorhouse, the band of the nearest regiment of the Irish army will escort you to the poorhouse door to the tune of St. Patrick's Day. *Oh! It will be nice to live in those days!*

"With the Green Flag floating o'er us" and an ever-increasing army of unemployed workers wulking about under the Green Flag, wishing they had something to eat. Same as now! Whoop it up for liberty!

Now, my friend, I also am Irish, but I'm a bit more logical. The capitalist, I say, is a parasite on industry; as useless in the present stage of our industrial development as any other parasite in the animal or vegetable world is to the life of the animal or vegetable upon which it feeds.

The working class is the victim of this parasite – this human leech, and it is the duty and interest of the working class to use every means in its power to oust this parasite class from the position which enables it to thus prey upon the vitals of labour.

Therefore, I say, let us organise as a class to meet our masters and destroy their mastership; organise to drive them from their hold upon public life through their political power; organise to wrench from their robber clutch the land and workshops on and in which they enslave us; organise to cleanse our social life from the stain of social cannibalism, from the preying of man upon his fellow man.

Organise for a full, free and happy life ***FOR ALL OR FOR NONE***.

Henry Charles had finally won all the boys over when, after a good scoop of *Glenmorangie*, recited the whole thing word for word.

A life lesson for all those intent on fulfilling the ideals of James Connolly.

And these boys were intent.

And Sandy C. watching bodies as they filed in the pub from a car that was used when out sniffing for the brew, knew that too. The *Black* knew it and wanted decisive action. Sandy C. did too just, a different type of action.

'Whores of the Empire'

Sandy C. was up early to walk the dog.
Hearts were up at Dens Park today and it
was essential to walk the dog and get
some porridge down early to start the day
on a good foundation. Sandy C. had
missed his tea last night so the porridge
(always salted never sugared) felt even
better this morning.

Sandy C. had been out last night on his
patrols. For years, he had been an expert
sniffer for the brew and had developed
many techniques of surveillance that had
worked wonders. People, he argued, were
creatures of habit and once you got to
know those habits, you got to know the
people. All their lives if they lived in the
same area (and most did) they drank in
the same pubs, punted in the same
bookies, shopped in the same shops,
smoked the same fags, caught the same
buses, talked to the same people and,
when they were all together, they

inevitably exchanged bodily fluids with each other.

Once Sandy C. realised all this, his job became a breeze and the easier it got, the more they paid him for it, allowing him to live outside the bubble of the underclass that he so despised. He had no truck with any form of so-called "Community". Thatcher was right. (Sandy C. would often tell his Brothers that Thatcher also said then that "there is no such thing as public money" He repeated it so often that the lads at the Masonic club got it printed up and framed for him which Sandy C. gratefully received and put up in the cubby hole of an office that he and Jimmy shared at High Riggs-Even that caused a stooshie as one of the guys had initially taken the picture to the Fenian framer at the bottom of Ferry Road and Junction Street which didn't go down well and was taken back a day later)

Sandy C. had seen it all. People claiming for things they were not entitled to, husbands claiming for their wives who were actually working, part or full time, illnesses signed off by weak doctors who didn't want the hassle of challenging the scrounger, people in a variety of disguises going to work whilst signing on, people who had built into their routines handing their sick line as much as going for a piss and the many, many people who had been moonlighting with a cash in hand job. Sandy C. wanted them all.

Last night, though, his targets were different.

'Beware of the risen people'

John was in *The Tango* post-Easter Road. Hibs had drawn 0-0 with Dundee Utd in front of a sparse crowd in freezing temperatures. Although he liked going to Easter Road, the fitba itself was dire and had been all season. There had been the presence of a mob from Dundee but a hardcore of *The Family* saw them off at the corner of Bothwell Street and Easter Road. Most of the boys headed north to their HQ in *The King Shot* but John had headed south and to the familiar terrain of *The Tango*. He had looked in *Frasiers* but had saw Billy the Hun in there and he wasn't quite ready for part two of *Daughtergate*.

The Tango wasn't too busy and there was no one in that John recognised saved for the bar staff. It was funny how staff carried themselves, an air of "we are better than you" emanating from them despite the fact they held jobs where you were paid from the neck down. John ordered his pint of lager and was going to have a seat, not fancying sharing small talk at the bar, when he spotted a familiar face walking from the toilets towards him. She cut a lonesome but elegant figure and had a nonchalance that belied her previous actions. On Hogmanay, John and she had slipped out the pub on the premise of securing a doner kebab among the scrum of people who were now beginning to disperse from the new year frivolities and John thought it was the optimum time to head to a kebab shop before the queue was akin to a Moscow *McDonalds.*

John and the girl, he'd found out as they dodged their way through the pished people that her name was Collette, got a kebab shop just at south bridge and the first thing John noticed was that the prices had almost doubled on account of the time of year. He cursed under his breath.

"Fur fucks sake"

Collette had already stridden forward and asked him what he wanted. He protested a bit, but she was insistent and ordering the full doner with everything on before he could really figure out what was going on. After putting the order in, Collette moved back to the steamy window that John was standing in front of in the shop and made small talk.

"Feels like a Tina Turner song this eh?"

John smiled then realised he hadn't a clue what Collette was talking about. She sensed this.

"On her new album, *Foreign Affair*, I got it at Christmas, there's a song on it, *Steamy Windows*, it's mega, like"

The penny dropped for John as he surveyed the scene. He also had a good look at Collette. She was tidy. He was pished but could still see he didn't need any inebriation to enhance her looks in his mind's eye. She was about 5,8, beautiful skin, blonde and eyes you could use as cufflinks. They had a lingering stare at each other before both breaking into a smile, both oblivious to the drunken revelry and, initially, not hearing the guy behind the counter shouting that their order was ready and Collette sloped over to collect it, turn, and land it in John's hands in what all seemed like one swift move.

They made their way out into the cold air like two hot dogs leaving a small oven in cinema and huddled together. John weighed up his options here. It was going to cost him Zimbabwe's national debt to get a taxi home and he wasn't overly keen on chaperoning the young lady to the reservation on the outskirts of the city where he called home. He had no idea what Collette's circumstances but pictured a cosy, wee flat with central heating and a comfy couch. As if reading his mind, Collette said:

"You want come back to my flat? It's in Dumbiedykes"

John nodded and said "Aye" as if the thought had never entered his head until now.

Collette grabbed John's jacket and veered him into one of Edinburgh's alleyways that also doubled as short cut between tourist Edinburgh and two-bit Edinburgh the tip of which was the huge monstrosity of flats that obscured *Arthur's Seat*, the extinct volcano that Robert Louis Stevenson described as *"a hill for magnitude, a mountain in virtue of its bold design"* but thankfully for John, and Collette for that matter, she had a cosy, wee flat that looked onto the high flats. Flats you could see from her comfy couch with a surround of heat provided by recently installed central heating.

It was upon entering the flat and sitting on said couch that John noticed, for the first time that whilst he was still holding his unopened and therefore, uneaten kebab, Collette had nothing.

"You no hungry? Or we sharing this?"

Collette, standing at the divide between kitchen and living room, paused for a little and replied:

"I'm hungry aye, but I am sharing fuckall"

'Whores of the Empire'

Vicky threw the dog a stick and then leisurely turned towards the water. It was still pitch black and bitterly cold, but she had her big coat on to protect her from the elements. There was no one else around save for one overly keen jogger, just visible on the boulevard of the beach as they (she couldn't tell if it was a man or a woman) jogged past the *Wimpy* and amusement arcade it made its home.

Vicky collected her thoughts. Time and tide wait for no man she thought as she looked into the water but what about women? It was at times like this she contemplated almost everything in her life, the bar, her weight, her trips to Belfast, her family and, of course, Sandy C.

She loved him and he was loyal but, occasionally, it went too far. She had indulged his sexual proclivities on the basis that she thought it would open him up a bit, make him less rigid. The reality was, she felt she was having to work harder and harder on making him more rigid. She smiled as the pun jogged through her mind.

Then it hit her.

Sandy C. had last penetrated her on May 2nd, 1986, the night before Hearts lost the league at Dens Park. Even at that, she had suspected that Sandy only wanted to get rid of as much of his bodily fluids as possible, so he had more space to quaff all the celebratory champagne that Wallace had ordered from the bar via a 25% lodge discount.

Sandy C. had sworn Vicky to secrecy about his new sexual wont and that was fine given that secrets were there thing. Vicky had hoped that Sandy C. and his new outlook would extend to holidays, but he stuck to his guns meaning that countries like Italy and Spain were out (Too many Catholics) Turkey was a no-

no (Never trust an Arab) and America, frankly, frightened Sandy C. due to its open arm policy on the Irish. *"An Irish bar on every corner"* may have sounded like heaven for many people but people like Sandy C. had vowed that would never happen in Scotland.

It was after Sandy C. had drunkenly ruminated this one night in his armchair that Vicky had an epiphany about her Cunt. Sandy C. was a strict once a week guy but the more she indulged his new needs, the less he took care of hers. That night, as he nodded his head slowly and pointed his finger to nowhere in particular, eyes half open, Vicky's mind started to wander. Sandy C. was then out cold as Vicky was red hot. Pushing her right into her black lace knickers, she was soon writhing in pleasure as she flicked her clitoris faster than an Orangeman could say *"No"* She plunged her index finger into her, now, wet ass pussy and dreamed of Sandy C. getting hard enough to sustain an erection.

Better yet, a younger man, one that was like low-hanging but forbidden fruit with the sort of junk hanging from him that could plunder her like a thief in an unlocked jewellers.

She climaxed on her hand, Sandy C. still out for the count.

The glistening sea reminding her of the glow from her hand as she removed it from her knickers,

Vicky snapped back into action as the dog had a retrieved the stick once again. Before throwing it she, like the rainbow, held it in her hand.

'Beware of the risen people'

Seany Beef was a minute late as he drove the van into the car park of the chapel. His whole family had been attending this chapel since before he could remember yet he still got butterflies when he saw the building and was alone.

He wasn't there to worship.

He was there to negotiate the procurement of the hall for a night in February so the Connolly boys could raise a few quid for the struggle over the water but things like this were never that simple. Seany had, what they call in these parts, *the gift of the gab.* He could talk himself out of the seemingly impossible situations and had been known to charm/irritate train ticket inspectors out of charging him for a ticket. Indeed, when a squad of the boys were arrested at a previous march, Seany had defended himself. The judge was so impressed that he gave 47 guilty verdicts and one not guilty.

He knocked on the door of the house next to the chapel and could hear Father Frank before he could see him such was the sound and ferociousness of Frank's cough. As the door bolt was opened, the smoke greeted Seany as if he was standing outside a steam room. Father Frank beckoned him in the door and through to the office that occasionally doubled as a kitchen.

There was an old oak table there with four chairs around it and Seany wasn't normally one for standing on ceremony or otherwise, so pulled a seat out from under the table and sat down. The chair was also wooden and felt cold. Father Frank put his cigarette out in an ashtray that he pulled from the dishes rack next to the sink.

"You maybe want to think about cutting doon on that smoking Frankie Five Angels"

Father Frank was unimpressed by Seany's baptism of him.

"What can I do for you Sean?" he said after taking a pew himself.

"Well, we wanted to book the hall for a celebration, 24th of February, Wee Benji, you ken wee Benji, he's 21 and, well, he's no had much in his life. He is one of the faith, Father, and I know you would never turn yer back on one of yer folk, Father"

Father Frank looked at Seany. He had an idea of who "Wee Benji" was and smelt something else was going on.

"Sean son, are you referring to Brendan McCart? He's from Gilmerton, he doesn't attend this parish? Does he even attend St John Vianney?"

Seany didn't skip a beat.

"Aye, well naw, whit happened is, mind he was here for my eldest nephew's christening last year? Well, he felt a sort of calling tae here Father and he's been looking for an excuse to come back so we thought, what better way, Father?"

Things like "Mass" went through Father Frank's head but Seany was moving in for the kill.

"You keep the bar, we will throw you a ton for incidentals and we will make sure the band are quiet when arriving and leaving"

Before Father Frank could say "Band? What Band?" Seany was up and shaking his hand.

"Cheers Frankie Five Angels and, listen, you get some *Vicks* on that chest of yours, the people of Leith need your sermons"

And with that, Seany was off.

'Whores of the Empire'

It had been a long day. The job centre was packed with people who had maybe worked over the Christmas period and then needed another job. There was a gloom about these people. 11 years of Thatcherism had battered the soul of the working classes to the point where there were no guarantees, no stability and no regular income.

There was a hopelessness among people over 30 in particular. They'd left school when Britain, they were told, was in turmoil and those who had turned 18 were encouraged to vote Conservative for a brighter more modern future.

The UK was a smaller country when she took power - 56.2m people lived here. That had been pretty stagnant since 1970, actually going down for four years before 1979 as the economy faltered. During the first years of Thatcher's reign, fewer people came to live in the UK -

acceptances for settlement went down from 69,670 in 1979 to 53,200 by 1990.

Ironically for a prime minister who focussed so much on family life, the 1980s saw the end of the traditional family unit for many. Divorce rates reached 13.4 per 1,000 married population in 1985.

As Britain learnt to come to terms with the idea of "no such thing as society", unemployment shot up under the Conservatives to levels not seen since the Great Depression.

Britain got hit by two major recessions under Thatcher, which sandwiched the boom of the 1980s but even that boom never saw GDP grow by more than a couple of percent.

Perceived wisdom is also that manufacturing disappeared under Thatcher. If so, it was something that had already started. In 1970, manufacturing accounted for 20.57% of UK GDP. By 1979 that was down to 17.62% of GDP. By the time she left office, that decline had continued - albeit at a slightly slower pace, down to 15.18%.

She may have been our first prime minister, but men still ended her decade paid a lot more than women.

Poverty went up under Thatcher, according to figures from the Institute for Fiscal Studies. In 1979, 13.4% of the population lived below 60% of median incomes before housing costs. By 1990, it had gone up to 22.2%, or 12.2m people, with huge rises in the mid-1980s.

With it came a huge rise in inequality. This shows the gini coefficient, which is the most common method of measuring inequality. Under gini, a score of one would be a completely unequal society; zero would be completely equal. Britain's gini score went up from 0.253 to 0.339 by the time Thatcher resigned.

However, there was one saviour for the masses-the weekend.

'Beware of the risen people'

As a man, it was always bizarre to be looking at the top of someone's head whilst they performed oral sex. The head would move up and down and the eyes would be transfixed on it. Occasionally, the head would come up so that the eyes could meet, still in performance. It's a strange to cast the act as performing or a *performance*. How do you rehearse it?

Can a woman, or man for that matter, say to a male friend:

 "I've got a date on Saturday night and I think I am going to be sucking his cock at some point in the evening, do you mind if I practice on yours?"

Also, if it is a performance, should the man critique? Give notes?

"Loved the way you approached it darling, very professional, four inches is a good length to begin with, but I'd like to see you build up to the full seven in your mouth within the first three minutes ok?"

Direction, does the man give it during performance?

"That's it, keep going at that pace then every 30 seconds or so take a nice, deep, stroke"

This also would suggest that the man receiving the gratification is in control. The person performing in the act is in total control if they know what they are doing. Having the ability to build up a rhythm not only takes control of the cock but the receivers mind as well.

Which is exactly what Collette had done to John in the seven minutes and 13 seconds between something exogenous being taken in the mouth, in this case John's cock, to liquid emission sliding down the oesophagus, in this case John's semen.

'Whores of the Empire'

Loyalism, for this was the word that encapsulated it all, had always been vibrant in Edinburgh but needed the pull of Belfast to provide the sprinkles of chocolate on top of the ice cream. Belfast was the heartland of the empire. People like Sandy C. had grown up with trips over the water. He had also seen the growth in younger people as their eyes lit up on their first visit as mural after mural filled their vision. The trips were important to show solidarity but equally important inn recruiting the next generation of Loyalist youth. You'd take them over on the boat, show them the sights, get them pished and get them laid by some middle-aged cougar who'd been denied a regular length on account of the length of a prison sentence doled out to their husband for committing an act of war like shooting an unarmed taxi driver or punters in a betting shop.

It was an interesting mindset at the heart of Loyalism. The Provisional IRA had its targets. Soldiers, certain politicians, collaborators with the British state and so on. Mistakes were made and, whatever the reasons for them, it was hard to justify them. There had also been cases where outrage seemed beyond faux when workers who were rebuilding a British Army base in Ireland were executed by the IRA. The public were appalled but the IRA were defiant:

"The IRA reiterates its long-standing call to those who continue to provide services or materials to the forces of occupation to desist immediately. Since 1985 the IRA has adopted a policy of taking military action aimed at ending Britain's cynical use of non-military personnel for the servicing and maintenance of British Crown Forces' bases and installations ... for our part, we in the IRA will not tolerate a situation where military personnel are freed from essential services and maintenance tasks and then

deployed where they can carry out wholesale repression within our community"

'Beware of the risen people'

Suggs Blacks was the place to be on a Saturday night in Edinburgh for young men to sample the best the city had to offer. Beautiful girls, cool music and a clientele that would have a good kick at stopping an invasion of Poland. *The Family* ran the place but even within that, there was a pyramid structure and right at the top of that was Luke Doyle. Not just because he was the hardest man around (There were a few others who had a decent shot at that title) but he also had the business acumen and ruthless streak required to run Edinburgh's number one night club. Luke had a name that transcended his years. From the age of around 3, he was already a well kent face in Edinburgh and had the sort of reputation that the Kray twins had by the time they got banged up.

As he moved up them football hooligan ranks, he moved more into making money and connections. By 16, he was a top boy in *The Family* and by 18 he had ownership of *Suggs Blacks* even if the name on the licence was one *David Glen Forbes*. There was no need for bouncers here as you'd need to be a on a suicide mission to start bother in there yet there was always the odd exception to the rule. There was also no dress code requirement like most other clubs. A policy they had taken directly from *The Hacienda* in Manchester.

As Shaun Ryder sang about being a simple city boy, with simple country tastes, Luke surveyed the scene of the club. There was the Ecstasy generation who flocked to the place on account of DJ's like *T-Haleygar* who was way ahead of all the other DJ's in Edinburgh with his fusion of indie and house music, illustrated by his current playing of track 1 from *Bummed* by Happy Mondays whilst most other clubs in Edinburgh were still playing Glenn Medeiros. There were the girls from public schools who had the cash, charisma and cool clientele air that made their presence a magnet for most of Edinburgh who had a penis. There was the generic young team posse who had aspirations of being Hibs Boys and saw patronising the club as a vital part of that ladder climb and then there was *The Family* themselves who could be seen at tables, laden with chilled bottled beers, in various numbers with lines of coke like poodles legs disappearing up the nostrils of guys who may have come from various parts of the city but came together at the weekends to form the hardest mob seen in Edinburgh since Cormack and *Protestant Action.*

Few people knew this, but Luke Doyle knew his history and was well acquainted with the politics of Edinburgh thanks to his close friendship with John Quinlivan. Plenty knew they were buddies but not many knew how close or what they talked about.

Both were highly intelligent men but, even more important than that, they were driven men who waited on no one. They knew the score. They both had the street smarts that could outwit a wily old urban fox, they were young, good looking and more articulate and knowledgeable than a taxi driver on *Mastermind*. They had long sessions where the talked politics, always from a working-class perspective, sociology, mental philosophy and events round the world as they happened. Yet people took them for thugs. Brains in their backside schemies who posed no threat to anyone never mind the establishment.

Of course, like any young working-class males in Edinburgh, they talked a lot of fitba, particularly the prospects of Hibernian Football Club, but also what was happening within the game in Scotland in general.

That's why, when he heard the chant go up, he knew exactly what the situation was.

Rangers were playing Dunfermline at East End Park that day. They'd won 1-0 thanks to a goal from Trevor Steven and *The Family* were well aware that on days like today, the Weegies who followed Rangers had to change trains in Edinburgh. They could do so at Haymarket but some, when full of drink, got the balls to come to Waverley. Rangers did have a firm, the ICC, but were laughed off by *The Family* on account of the fact that the stupid cunts had stolen their name from West Ham. It didn't even make sense as it stood for Inter City Crew and was a nod to the fact that the West Ham firm travelled first class on public trains to blend in with other, non-football, commuters and not on the cattle trains provided by the polis and called "Football Specials". The Rangers version of the ICC couldn't spell 'first class' and wanted to be seen and heard on every train they stepped where, seemingly, every other passenger was a 'Fenian Bastard'

The commotion being caused across *Suggs Browns* dance floor wasn't down to the ICC though. Two jokers wearing Rangers scarves, *Pepe* jeans and Rugby style sweatshirts were mithering women on the dance floor, waving their scarves like helicopter propellers and trying out sing *The Charlatans* with their inebriated version of *Derry's Walls* a song that commemorates the 'Siege of Derry' and is sung, aptly, to the tune of 'God Bless the Prince of Wales'.

T-Haleygar had seen the disturbance and quickly flipped tracks from *The Only One I Know* to a track he had got an early sample of before its release, The Only Rhyme That Bites which, even in the melee, reminded him he had an invitation to the album release of *Northern Heights by MC Tunes*, where the track came from, on June 1st. The track was a collaboration with *808 State* and intensified the atmosphere of the club from the previous Ecstasy fuelled trance it had been in.

As good as the track was, it didn't intensify the atmosphere as much as Luke Doyle calmly walking across the dance floor did. He had already signalled to the eager eyes watching from a table that he had the situation under a control with a simple waving of his right hand further to the right being the signal that no one had to leap across the table and exterminate the two Hun cunts as if they were rats who were scampering across the kitchen floor as your wife and mother stood on chairs, screaming.

They two Rangers supporters continued to cavort, completely unaware that the *Enola Gay* was heading straight for them.

At this point, the taller of the two spotted Luke Doyle and asked, sneeringly, what the fuck he was looking at? When Doyle continued to eyeball him, the drunken dancer swung a punch that was calmly, and easily, avoided by Doyle as if he was sparring with one of those punch bags you stood on after you had gotten it for a gift at Christmas when you were 8 years old. The second sauced swinger saw this and aimed a head but at Luke Doyle that he simply took one step back to avoid.

As *MC Tunes* sang 'My knees began a knocking' Luke Doyle swung a right hand then left and knocked the two Rangers chocolates spark out. Before *MC Tunes* has got through the American states, the two guys were dragged out the back door and left on Waverley Bridge, still unconscious, but alive and taken for two pissed up clowns but the night time revellers.

Which was pretty much spot on.

'Whores of the Empire'

The cheeriness of a bright and sunny
Sunday morning in Leith was replaced
with a quizzical air as the people entering
the Edinburgh Masonic Club peered at
Alan Phillips and Davie Robb. The two
of them didn't really look like each other,
Alan was tall, slim and had the look of
Hen Broon without the moustache about
him. Davie was stocky, well-built and
looked Joe Bugner to the more discerning
eye.

There was nothing out of ordinary about
Edinburgh's top Loyalists meeting for a
friendly curer pint on a Sunday in the
Masonic Club, but things were different
today as Alan and Davie looked like
twins of a kind as they sat at the round,
light brown, varnished table with a pint
of *Tennents* and a pint of *Export* in front
of them. Willie Pullar, a barman in the
club for over 40 years, had served the
pints, observed the injuries but had said
fuck all.

Jimmy was just in front of Sandy C. as the latter liked to lock the front door after they entered because it was still a good 90 minutes away from the legal Sunday opening time of half 12.

Jimmy looked at the pair of them and did a double take. Alan had a black left eye and Dougie had a black right eye.

"Fuck me, it's the Black and White Minstrel show"

And burst out laughing.

Neither Davie nor Alan replicated.

Jimmy shouted over to Willie for a large whiskey and half pint of lager just as Sandy C. appeared and ordered a half of *Export* and a double *Bells*.

It was only as he sat down, letting out a sigh, that he noticed the black eyes looking right at him.

"Fuck me, did you two walk into a revolving door?"

Again, neither Alan nor Davie laughed.

Sandy C. could see they weren't in a jovial mood.

Pulling up a chair, he tried to engage them again:

"So, what happened boys?"

Sandy C. looking at Davie then Alan then back to Davie as if to make sure they still had the injuries.

Alan started, ironically, as if he was a witness in court.

"We went to the Rangers game at East End Park. Got the train from Haymarket, over there in no time, got off at Dunfermline Queen Margaret and settled into the *Elizabethan* pub on Halbeath Road.

Sandy C. and Jimmy nodded in acknowledgment at the recognition of both the pub name and location.

"The pub was teeming with Bluenoses and we ended up having a good scoop with a few Brothers from Linwood. Anyway, we ended up at the game with them. The game wasn't up to much, but Trevor Steven bailed us out with a peach of a goal"

Sandy C. and Jimmy both thought to themselves "Jammy Cunts"

"Anyway, we went back to the boozer with the Linwood boys, had a few more scoops and jumped on the train back to Edinburgh. This one here-

Alan looked at Davie.

-says we should bypass Haymarket, scoot on in to the toon"

Both Sandy C. and Jimmy noticed that first change to vernacular, their DHSS training kicking in.

"I wasn't sure. We weren't dressed and had colours on, but Davie insisted so the next thing, we are off the train at Waverley and heading up the stairs towards Market Street.

"At first, we were going to head straight up to the High Street, but I didn't fancy the stairs given how cunted I was and how out of breath the stairs in the station had made me so, instead, we turned right and stumbled on that *Suggs Blacks* place. There was nae cunt on the door and we just steamed in. I spotted a couple of gorgeous birds on the dance-floor and we started dancing with them. They were intae it like. We were just dancing wi them, minding our own business. Then, oot of nowhere, I got punched from the back and Davie did as well. Next thing I know, two Polis are waking us up on Waverley Bridge and offering us both a lift home. They were Brothers. I woke up this morning and I fucking realised who had sucker punched the both of us. It was that cunt Doyle who hings aboot wi Quinlivan"

This information startled both Jimmy and Sandy C.

This had gone from a laugh about drunken debauchery to an attack on two of Edinburgh's most prominent Loyalists.

They looked at each other, knowing exactly what the other was thinking, without saying a word, holding the look until Sandy C. gave Jimmy the slightest of nods.

With that, Jimmy turned to Davie, who hadn't said a word yet such was his anger and indignation at what happened the night before.

"Davie, you mentioned the guys from Portadown and Belfast a couple of weeks ago at the *Black* meeting?"

This made Davie sit up.

"You still in touch…?"

To be continued…

Printed in Great Britain
by Amazon